JUN 1 1 2012

# AD ETERNUM

# AD ETERNUM

## Elizabeth Bear

Subterranean Press 2012

**First Edition**

**ISBN**
978-1-59606-444-7

Subterranean Press
PO Box 190106
Burton, MI 48519

**www.subterraneanpress.com**

*When we've been here ten thousand years*
*bright shining as the sun.*
*We've no less days to sing God's praise*
*than when we've first begun.*
—"Amazing Grace"


Hymn originally by John Newton (1779),
additional verse first recorded by Harriet Beecher Stowe
after an African-American oral tradition (1852).
Believed to have been adopted from another hymn,
entitled "Jerusalem, My Happy Home." (1790)

**New Amsterdam, New Netherlands,**
*United Democratic States of North America.*
**March, 1962**

# 1.

THE WAMPYR CALLED HIMSELF Jack Prior.

It was just a name, the latest of hundreds. A memorial, though almost no one alive would understand it. He had newly adopted it, to mark the end of yet another existence.

That he wore it on his first return in the span of a human life to New Amsterdam was merely the sort of ironic coincidence that one came to appreciate—to anticipate—in an existence bounded only by your tolerance for loss.

Travel was easier than the last time the wampyr had crossed the Atlantic. Then, it had meant weeks aboard ship or days in a dirigible. Now, it could be managed in a night, if you were willing to accept certain risks—risks which could be minimized by the careful selection of one's airline.

The wampyr arranged his travel through a carrier headquartered in London. He embarked immediately upon completion of the state funeral for Dame Commander Abigail

Irene Garrett, the legendary matriarch of the Crown's Own, which had been held at the Enchancery after sunset. Such unconventional timing was out of unstated deference for those mourners who could not bear the light of the sun.

A lifespan in excess of a century was enough time to accumulate a great many strange friends.

It raised another irony—perhaps delicious, perhaps merely bittersweet—that despite the wampyr's general lack of enthusiasm for mortal politics (or immortal ones, for that matter), it was the gratitude of politicians that made his travel so easy. In no small part due to his activities during the Great War, English aeroplanes were equipped to carry passengers of the blood. Sections of the cabin could be shielded by blackout curtains should the sun rise in transit.

It wasn't *discreet*, but it wasn't as if it were exactly illegal to be a wampyr in America anymore. Inconvenient, certainly. But the wampyr was inured to inconvenience.

The wampyr spent the long flight reading a lightly fictionalized account of a young soldier's experiences with the American and Iroquois forces sent to relieve Pavelgrad during the Great War—and, when that grew too depressing, with knitting a particularly intricate pair of socks. The book—and the socks—aided him in pretending oblivion to the occasional curious glances of his fellow passengers.

The airliner chased the dark across the Atlantic, and in the cold of late winter there was plenty of dark to embrace it. He had no need to draw the curtains, and the stewardess had been kind enough to seat him by himself, so the nauseating smells from the other passengers' dinners afflicted him less than they might.

It was the wampyr's first experience in such an aircraft, and he could not help but compare it to the luxuries of an airship or passenger liner. The seats seemed comfortable—it was hard for him to tell, who required so little comfort now—and the stewardesses were attentive. He understood without asking that they were very like rail conductors or the stewards on ocean liners: the passengers might believe that the attendants were there to see to their needs, but their most pressing purpose was crowd control.

He found it a curiously comforting revelation. The technology changed, but the people and the purposes it served were unaltering. There was something very pleasant about the long, dark cylinder full of rustling, sleeping mortals—like a stable at night, or a cote full of dozy pigeons. He turned and gazed out the window, watching the stark beams of a swollen moon glance off the moving water.

New Amsterdam was a dazzle of lights out of the starboard windows as the metal bird dipped a wing and banked towards its final approach. The wampyr, seated by the window, turned to gaze out it as a tall man stopped beside his row.

He'd known the stranger was coming down the aisle, known that he was about to stop. He'd read the man's intentions in the slightly accelerating heartbeat and conscious tenseness of his breath as he came up, and if there had been any scent of aggression, the wampyr would have made the usual tiresome preparations to defend himself. But while the stranger smelled of apprehension and his breathing indicated nervousness, there was nothing about him that would suggest he meant the wampyr harm.

"I'm Dr. Damian Thomas," he said. The brush of fabric told the wampyr he had extended a hand. Over the tang of nervousness, he smelled clean and well-fed, a scent laced with the grassiness of some modern cologne. "May I sit?"

The wampyr turned. Dr. Thomas was indeed quite tall, stooped beneath the overhead bulkhead in a charcoal-gray Savile Row suit. He was not slender, like many tall men, but broad-shouldered and well-proportioned. A faint overtone of English university overlaid an accent the wampyr would place as mid-Atlantic American.

The knitting needles rested in the wampyr's lap; he wasn't wearing gloves, and in the warmth of the aircraft, neither was the other man.

Well, if he wasn't going to pretend to be something he wasn't, he couldn't hold the curiosity of living men against them. It was a new world. In more ways than one.

"John Prior," he said, and extended his fingers. "Call me Jack. Suit yourself."

Dr. Thomas's hand was ink-spotted and warm, the back brown as coffee-berries and the palm a yellow tan. He didn't react to the dry-stick neutrality of the wampyr's touch, confirming that it came as no surprise.

"My pleasure." He seated himself, sliding a small carry-on bag beneath the seat.

The wampyr began tucking his book and his knitting away. "Medical doctor?"

"Doctor of Thaumaturgy," Dr. Thomas said. "Oxford, '57. And what do you do?"

Before he remembered himself, the wampyr said, "I'm a private detective."

"I thought you might be." Dr. Thomas left it at that—*I know who you are, and I respect your desire for privacy.* A gold ring on his right hand glinted as he fastened his seatbelt.

The wampyr wondered, *Widowed?*

"I noticed you were reading Vonnegut. Any good?"

*The blood are only so strong as their courts,* the wampyr reminded himself.

"Troubling," he said. "But not untrue."

They said the aeroplane "touched down," but it was nothing like the feather-soft alighting of an airship. Instead, the wheels struck tarmac and bounced up—not hard, but hard enough that the wampyr set a hand against the back of the seat before him. Electric floodlights glazed the rough ground rushing at incredible speeds beneath the landing gear. Banks of dirty snow littered brown earth along the runway's edges.

"Well," Dr. Thomas said. "Survived another one. Is this your first time in New Amsterdam?"

"I haven't been back in a long time," the wampyr answered. It was the sort of non-answer that became second nature after a few hundred years, and spared explanations—and even if you weren't trying to hide what you were, it did not take very long at all for those explanations to become excruciatingly tedious. "I imagine everything has changed."

Dr. Thomas reached into his breast pocket and offered a card. "Perhaps we can be of service to one another at some point. Please do keep in touch."

"Perhaps." The wampyr slipped the card into his pocket. "I'm afraid I can't yet return the favor—but in the interim, I can be contacted via the Hotel Aphatos."

Dr. Thomas's eyebrow rose. "I see."

"I did not think you would be surprised."

"Not…surprised. Or rather, not shocked. Or outraged. But perhaps a little surprised that you are so willing to trust a stranger."

"I have nothing to hide," said the wampyr. After a few moments too long, he remembered that this was when he was supposed to smile.

And to keep his lips closed.

—⁓—

When the wampyr last resided in this city, there had been no such institution as the Hotel Aphatos. He had been the only one of his kind in New Amsterdam; possibly the only one in all the English possessions in the New World. He had come here for a fresh start then, as well.

Perhaps it was a pattern. It was hard to avoid repetition, after the first few hundred years.

Now New Amsterdam had a club devoted to serving the special needs of the blood, and that would make the wampyr's transition back to residency simpler. But before he went to the hotel, he had other matters to attend to.

As the passengers crossed the tarmac to the gate, the wampyr noticed a number of men and women gathered behind wooden sawhorses, presumably awaiting their loved ones or those to whom they felt a duty. However, there were a few others whose ready cameras and elongated notepads set them apart.

*I am anticipated*, he thought, even as the first cries of "Doctor Chaisty!" and "Don Sebastien!" reached his ears.

"Pardon me," the wampyr said in excuse to his temporary traveling companion. As the first camera flashed, he stepped out of line and let himself fade into the darkness. Ignoring the passenger walkways, he moved with speed around the waiting crowd—before they were even sure what had happened—and toward the exits.

He had no luggage—he had shipped trunks ahead. When he saw the line of picketers arrayed near baggage claim, he was grateful to have avoided it. They carried signs bearing such legends as Blood For The Living and God Hates Vamps.

It was a step up from mobs armed with torches and farm implements. He would have preferred to arrive unheralded, but it appeared he had reckoned without the good offices of the Transatlantic cable.

He found a checkered taxi at the stand in front of the airport. The hack—a slick-haired Italian who hid a copy of Mary Wollstonecraft's *The Modern Prometheus* under a half-completed crossword puzzle—loaded the wampyr's carry-on in the boot...in the *trunk*.

Seated in the back, the wampyr paused before giving the driver directions to an address fronting Jardinstraat. "On the island of Manhattan."

The hack's glance in his rearview mirror told the wampyr that his specificity was unwarranted. "Nice address. Just let me get through this mess..."

The protestors, apparently having determined that their quarry had eluded them, spilled into the drive near the doors from baggage claim. The wampyr noted that they did not adhere to the marked pedestrian crossing zones.

The wampyr leaned back and closed his eyes. "What's going on?"

"Some famous vamp supposedly coming in from England or something," the hack said. His shirt rasped on vinyl as his shoulders rose and fell against the seat. "It was in the *Manhattanite*."

That was a new paper. The wampyr had been familiar with the morning papers—the *New Amsterdam Courant* and the *New World Times*—and the afternoon papers, the *Record* and the *Gazette*.

"No doubt the very nonpareil of reasoned journalism," the wampyr said.

The hack snorted. "It's got the best comics, what can I say."

"Wait—" the wampyr said, holding a hand across the back of the driver's seat. "—take me through the city. Please."

"First time in New Amsterdam?"

The wampyr didn't answer, just leaned away and turned his head to gaze outside. He stretched his shoulders against the seatback and cracked the window so he could scent the night air. "Just have me at the house by five a.m."

Wistfully, the hack said, "There's a great spot to watch the sun come up over the Hudson Channel Bridge—"

"Maybe next time," the wampyr answered. "Tonight, just take me up the Boston Post Road."

To his credit, the hack didn't bring it up again. He drove the wampyr through a city made strange by time— yet in some ways eerily familiar. The Boston Post was the only road on Manhattan that stretched from tip to tip without interruption, and they drove the length of it—from the green meadows and parkland of the Bowery to the wild rising of the thorny hills at the island's apex. Between, the moon and the stars went invisible behind streetlights and tall buildings.

When the wampyr had dwelt here last, it was rare to find a structure over seven stories—and the tallest had been twenty-two or twenty-three, laden with such modern conveniences as lifts and electricity. It was strange to see them dwarfed, now—the elegant ivory silhouette of the Flatiron Building overshadowed by towers four times its height, floodlights blazing along their sides to paint their silhouettes in stark reverse against the darkness.

Even in the hour of the wolf, the streets were not deserted. Nor were they crowded, in particular, but a few individuals drifted along the sidewalks, and a few automobiles glided through the light-stippled streets. New Amsterdam was like London, like Paris in that regard: she might not sleep, but she dozed as fitfully as the passengers on the airliner had.

The hack turned his collar up but didn't complain about the open window, for which the wampyr was glad. Because the scents that flooded in on the late-winter air were likewise familiar and strange.

The wampyr was given to understand that mortals could not smell the sea from within Manhattan's rack of streets and towers. He could, though, and the rank tang of the oil that clotted it. He could smell the garbage, the greasy putrescence of cooking food, the blood that whispered so close beneath the skin of men and women and stray dogs slinking along the city's sidewalks.

"Gorgeous," he whispered.

Equally hushed, the hack replied, "I love this shift."

When the cab dropped the wampyr in front of the house on Jardinstraat, the wampyr paid the hack double and told him to leave the meter running and go watch the sunrise. His block had changed very little: the long row of tidy townhouses with their iron banisters and winter-gray planters still snuggled between much taller, modern buildings on either side.

The sky was still indigo behind the wash of city lights as the cab pulled away, leaving the wampyr standing on a sidewalk at the end of the block, before a dark townhouse with its shades drawn and its steps—which described a graceful curve from sidewalk to a corner door—impeccably swept. The planters on either side had been weeded and trimmed back for winter, and the wampyr was pleased to see the thin green blades of crocus leaves gliding up from the compost that filled them.

At the top of the steps, he turned and looked back out at Jardinstraat Park. From this vantage, he could see over the low wall that bounded it. Water glinted behind a screen of bare trees; the winter's ice on the reservoir had melted. The scents of cold earth and sap stirring reached him.

The key was in his pocket.

He opened the door of 184 Jardinstraat and let himself inside.

The house where he had lived another lifetime smelled of lemon polish and uninhabitation. He'd hired caretakers and housekeepers, and it seemed they had not taken advantage of their employer's absence to let the house deteriorate. But neither had fires been laid in its hearths for more than half a century. No sunlight had fallen across its carpets, or the upholstery of its sheet-covered chairs. It was as clean and empty as a museum exhibit of life in the 19<sup>th</sup> century.

The wampyr locked the door behind himself. Normally he would have come in through the side entrance with its small mudroom, rather than standing here in the echoing foyer. But there were times to stand on ceremony, and a sort of homecoming after almost sixty years away seemed one of them.

The wampyr set the small bag with his knitting and book beside the door. With slow steps, he paced from room to room, reacquainting himself with the house. He trailed a hand over the dustless surfaces of mantel and the long dining room table where DCI Garrett had once performed a magic trick. As gray morning crept in through the shades drawn over tight-closed windows, he climbed the central stair and looked into each room. All was in order. All was as he and Jack had left it when they had fled to Boston, and from there to Paris.

It wasn't like a museum, he realized. It *was* a museum. A museum of a world that was dead.

He wondered what the neighbors had thought of this house that stayed vacant—but well-maintained—as property values skyrocketed around it, as its sister townhouses were sold off one by one and modern buildings three times taller skyrocketed, too.

He would need to hire servants. Trustworthy ones, probably through the auspices of the club. He'd see to it— and start the process—after sundown. In the meantime, however...well, the dead did not sleep.

He imagined all his books were where he'd left them.

In his ascent, he finally reached the sixth floor and the servant's quarters. These rooms had not been so well-maintained: they were clean, but not aired. It had probably never occurred to the maintenance workers that anyone would care to check them, except the people who would be living here and cleaning them themselves.

He would have central heating installed. Electricity. Though he did not require such things himself.

Slowly, he descended. As the sun rose behind the towers all around, it was growing too bright in the front room now to be comfortable despite the window shades. The wampyr's study was dim and comfortable. It had always been his daytime sanctuary. He fetched his knitting and pulled a battered Baroness Orczy from the shelf beside the fireplace. An ornately gilt-framed mirror—an Alexandrian excrescence that had been the height of English fashion when New Amsterdam was still a city in a colony—hung above the black marble mantel.

The wampyr no more reflected in its silvered glass than he would in a crashing waterfall. He reached out and pressed his fingertips to it anyway. Its chill felt neutral against the dry flesh of his fingertips.

"Jack Prior."

His voice sounded dusty in his own ears.

"Yes," he said. "I am Mr. Prior. Pleased to meet you."

# 2.

THE HOTEL APHATOS WAS on the far side of the Jardinstraat Park from the wampyr's house, and quite a bit south. Still, it wasn't so far that the wampyr hesitated to walk it, once the direct light of the sun had faded. By then, even he was somewhat restless—and the passage of centuries had left him with a stock of patience that would serve the envy of any hunting cat.

In the chill of evening he shrugged on overcoat and gloves and tugged a hat onto his head. He wouldn't feel the cold, but scandal attended those who went about in their shirtsleeves in the wintertime. Even as he locked the door behind himself, he mocked his own caution at keeping up appearances: here he was about to intentionally walk through the front door of a wampyr club without so much as a subterfuge.

*Either you're in or you're out*, he told himself.

The walk required half an hour at a leisurely pace. He paused on the sidewalk before the Hotel Aphatos and looked up at the discreetly calligraphed sign above its violet awnings. As he'd half-expected, a crowd of three or four young men with short hair and cheap coats stood around, holding placards aloft in one gloved hand while warming the other in the opposite armpit.

The Aphatos was a new building constructed to look old. The pale gray façade rose above the street in ornate tiers and a doorman in scarlet guarded the entry, and the protestors stood well back from him. As the wampyr turned on the sidewalk to approach the entrance, however, the broadest of the young men broke away from the group. Egged on by the catcalls of his friends, he approached.

The wampyr did not turn to look. He did not alter his course. If an attack came, he was ready; if it did not, the young man was beneath his notice.

To his surprise, another young man, this one bearded and wearing a vest that said ESCORT over threadbare clothing, stepped between the wampyr and the protestors.

"You may not block access to private property," he said, as if he recited it a thousand times a day.

"Prior," the wampyr said to the doorman. "I'm expected."

"Of course, sir," said the doorman, and swept the door aside.

The lobby might not have seemed out of place in any hotel. The windows, though tinted, were not obscured—those windows faced east, and their awnings would keep direct sun from spilling across the brown-and-tawny marble floor for most of the day. In the early mornings, when the sun rose across Jardinstraat Park, the light could be blocked by Japanese screens. In the afternoons and evenings, the hotel's wampyr denizens could take their ease in overstuffed leather chairs and enjoy the track of the light across the trees—and the leaves and grass, in such seasons as offered some.

For now, what lay beyond the plate glass was the protestors, the escort, a few hurried pedestrians…and the prowling sweep of automobile lights along the street. The wampyr turned away.

He presented himself to the concierge, who was mortal and unruffled, and asked if there was any mail or any messages. "Prior," he said. "John. Or Jack."

Each time, it came out easier. It always took more time to wear in a new name than to wear out an old.

While the concierge checked the cubbies, the wampyr wondered if he would find anyone he knew from a past life in residence.

"Here you are, sir," the concierge said, returning with a scant handful of envelopes. "Will you be staying in the hotel?"

"I maintain a residence in the city." The wampyr restrained himself from flipping through return addresses—for now. "I will require access to the club, however."

"Of course," said the concierge. "You'll find it on the mezzanine. And should you require a room for the day—" he tipped his head eloquently "—those are easily made available."

"Thank you." The wampyr tipped the concierge, then took his mail aside and began opening envelopes. Most were simply business matters, as his regular correspondents had known of his imminent change of address since Abby Irene had entered her final illness. But one was on thick, creamy laid paper and had the feel of an invitation. There was no postmark. It must have been hand-delivered.

The wampyr set his hat on the arm of the chair and slit the flap with a fingernail. A cold draft drew his attention; the doorman had admitted two willowy young women dressed in straight-skirted dresses that ended well above the knee. They smelled warm, appetizing—but over even the smell of blood and life lay the gloss of extreme youth. They giggled and leaned together, brown-haired and round-armed and underdressed for the weather.

The wampyr slid the card from the envelope.

It was an invitation to a party at a good address in Groenwijck for that very night after eight. The hostess's name was Sarah Emrys; the wampyr had not heard of her. The lingering smell of ink and a woman's hand encouraged him to turn the card over.

On the back, in elegant penmanship, a woman had written in blue: *I apologize for the lateness of this invitation, but I had only just heard from my dear friend Dr. Thomas that you have arrived in New Amsterdam. I do hope you can join us.*

The wampyr glanced at the bank of lifts and the curving stair leading to the mezzanine. He heard the giggle of the two young women daring each other further into the hotel. He thought of awkward fumblings in rented rooms, and the necessity of small talk afterwards, and the nearly inevitable discovery that neither party in the transaction was really what the other had fantasized.

He wasn't that hungry.

He checked his watch: a little before 7. He wondered if there was still time to send an R.S.V.P. The note seemed to indicate no need for one, but the habits of politeness had become much ingrained.

The invitation had a telephone number. It would be easy enough to ask the concierge to call while the wampyr found himself a cab. At least he was already dressed for evening.

The wampyr arranged to be fashionably late. Another building, another doorman, another marble lobby—this one white and veined brown like old ice. Miss Emrys' flat was on the ground floor. The doorman inspected the wampyr's invitation and showed him the way.

The space beyond the solid oaken door was filled with heartbeats and voices, the warm smell of living women and living men. He rapped and waited.

Quick heel-clicking footsteps rattled on a hard-wood floor. The door opened a crack, revealing a strip of peach party dress with ash-brown hair falling over one shoulder, and rattled to the end of a chain that was far less defense against the wampyr's entrance than the word of the woman whose pale fingers curled around the frame.

The wampyr held the invitation up. "Prior," he said. "Miss Emrys, I presume?"

"Of course." Excitement and anxiety sharpened her scent. "How good of you to come."

She shut the door long enough to wiggle the chain loose, then opened it wide. She stood aside, obviously expecting him to answer.

The wampyr smiled at her gently, with closed lips. "Weren't you going to invite me in?"

"Oh," she said. "Of course! Please come in." She laughed. "Enter freely, and of your own will."

He bowed in an intentionally archaic fashion, handed her his hat, and stepped within.

Food smells assaulted him, but he was too experienced to show his distaste. Instead, he waited for his hostess to shut the door and hang his hat—and the coat he also surrendered—then turn back to him. The flat was large enough to boast a kind of foyer or front hall dominated by a blazing fireplace framed in dark wood paneling. A corridor led off to the left, and the wampyr assumed that the kitchen and bedrooms were that way. Glass French doors stood open off the hallway where he stood. In clockwise order, they led to a dining room, parlor, and a library.

The food smells wafted from the dining room—but in defiance of the customary mechanics of parties, the sounds and laughter were concentrated in the library.

"This way, Mr. Prior," Miss Emrys said.

"Jack," he said.

She looked at him, shocked or perhaps merely a little taken aback. "Jack?"

"Call me Jack," he said, and allowed her to take his elbow and lead him across the hall.

Setting aside Miss Emrys, four people were gathered within. The wampyr was not too surprised to note that one of them was Dr. Thomas. Of the others, one was a man and two women. The man and one of the women were of apparent European lineage; the second woman had glossy black hair grown long, in a single straight fall cut blunt across the bottom, and the ochre skin of the native American peoples. She wore her years with a mature handsomeness.

The white woman was nondescript in a beige suit, leading the wampyr to fear that unless she demonstrated unusual strength of character, she was destined to remain to him *the other one*. The man was fortyish and of average height, with a little paunch insufficiently concealed by a waistcoat that matched his silk suit and his balding brown hair cut close against the sides of a roundish skull. His shirt cuffs were shot to show black coral links. As he appraised the wampyr, the wampyr experienced the brief familiar sensation that he was being sized up as a threat.

"Welcome to my little salon," said Miss Emrys. "Mr. Jack Prior, you already know Dr. Damian Thomas. This is Dr. Ruthanna Wehrmeister—"

She grinned at the wampyr as he raised her hand, an honestly entertained smirk that took her age from nondescript, but not old, to youthful and full of mischief. "Mr. Prior. So your ancestors were preachers?"

"I'm not sure," he said. "Were yours combat sorcerers?" The decades in London had stood him in good stead; his skin, even given a wampyr's pallor, might be swarthy for an Englishman, but no trace of the foreign or archaic remained in his accent now.

Dr. Wehrmeister laughed out loud, no polite girlish trill but something hearty and spontaneous. "Not mine," she said, with a nod to the older, probably-Iroquois woman. "But Mrs. Blacksnake here is the granddaughter of the great Seneca general Halftown. It is likely she that should carry the sobriquet 'war-master,' since her grandfather's sorceries held the Iroquois line against the British for thirty years."

"Please," said Mrs. Blacksnake. "He had help. And you must call me Estelle."

"I did not know," the wampyr said, with what he hoped was politeness, "that the Iroquois had taken to adopting European names."

"Only when we deal on a regular basis with our thick-tongued friends," she said tolerantly.

"Of course," the wampyr said. Then, embarrassed that it had taken so long for him to come to the understanding, he added, "I've fallen into a nest of sorcerers."

It explained why such a diverse group would be gathered together, when the wampyr understood that the United Democratic States of North America were still largely socially segregated in ways mysterious to a European.

"Indeed you have," said Dr. Thomas. "I hope you don't mind."

The wampyr seated himself. "Some of my dearest friends have been sorcerers," he said wryly. He turned to the last unintroduced man and extended his still-gloved hand. "Good afternoon, sir."

"Mr. Prior," said Sarah Emrys. "May I present the Prince Ragoczy, late of Kyiv."

The wampyr did not raise his brows. —A pleasure, he said in Russian. —I am afraid my Ukrainian is rather dusty. I hope this approximation does not offend.—

"Not at all," said the Prince. "Your consideration is noted."

By the thinning of his hair and the pores in his cheeks, the wampyr would have placed him as a man in his forties, and fond of his drink. But he moved like someone younger.

"So," the wampyr said. "You are the Comte de St. Germain. How very odd to meet you after all these years."

"I beg your pardon?" said Ragoczy.

"I recognize the name you are using." The wampyr sat back. "But I was in Paris in the seventeen fifties, and I do not think I saw *you* there."

Dr. Wehrmeister sat back with her hands in the lap of her skirted suit. One of Mrs. Blacksnake's eyebrows rose.

"How curious," said the Prince. "Because while I will admit that a powdered wig hides many sins, I daresay I recollect *you*, Monsieur Gosselin."

# 3.

IT WAS NOT AN easy task to rescue a conversation in a small group from such an inauspicious beginning, but Mrs. Blacksnake managed it. As challenging stares passed between the wampyr and the man he considered an impostor, the Seneca sorceress threw back her head and rasped a smoker's complicated laugh.

"Fantastic!" she said, when she'd slowed down a little. "We haven't had a good bitter rivalry in months!"

She nudged Dr. Wehrmeister, who glanced at her and forced a chuckle.

Dr. Wehrmeister sipped her tea and made a face. "If there's going to be a duel," she said in her delicate accent, "I for one want a brandy."

When she leaned forward, the eyelet lace at the edges of her blouse gaped slightly, showing the symbols inked above her sternum. Alchemical marks, tattooed in crimson.

"No duel," said the wampyr. Without touching, he gestured with a gloved hand to the notch of her collarbone, then down. "Sorbonne?" he guessed.

Smiling, she shook her head.

"I'll fetch the brandy anyway," Miss Emrys said. It was becoming rapidly evident that this was not her first salon, because she was back in a flash—with a decanter decorated with roses and mismatched tumblers for everyone, even the wampyr. This must be the new shabby-Bohemian chic he'd been hearing about. The patterns might be random, but the crystal was still leaded, and it caught the glow of the electric lights like prisms.

"Thank you," he said. "But don't waste good brandy on me." Gently, he nudged the empty cut crystal away with his fingertips.

She blanched. "Oh, I am so terribly sorry—"

"Don't be." He smiled generously, because he could. "I don't know what I'm missing."

"A great deal," said the man who called himself Ragoczy. "But never mind. I do not require that you believe me. Only that you entertain me. After all, is that not what we are here for?"

Miss Emrys poured brandy quickly, stiff measures with articulate hands. She passed the glasses and kept one for herself.

"So you gather here to discuss magic?" the wampyr said. "Miss Emrys, may I ask where you studied?"

"Sarah, please."

He nodded. "I know your line of old—"

"I have no spark," she said sadly. "But—as you intimated—I was raised in a family of sorcerers, and I find

I prefer their company. One need not practice magic to theorize." She kissed her fingers in self-mocking farewell.

She continued, "Of course Estelle was educated in her family. Damian—" he smiled in acknowledgement, cupping his hands around the glass so it vanished "—at Oxford. The Prince was educated in Kyiv. Ruthanna's provenance, or *Provence*—" Groans around the room told the wampyr that what Sarah Emrys lacked in spark, she made up for in terrible puns "—you have already failed to determine."

"I am one of America's first native-educated doctors of Thaumaturgy," Dr. Wehrmeister said. "Schooled at Yale. As a matter of fact, I studied under Doctor…with Damian. Who is that institution's first Black professor of Thaumaturgy."

The wampyr said, "I had no idea I was being invited to such a rarified gathering."

"Ah," said Emrys—Sarah. She looked at Ruthanna. "Well…"

"It was my idea," Damian said. "I'll explain."

There was a time when the wampyr would have picked up the glass, just to fidget with it. Now, he folded his hands across his knees and let the stillness take him. He could all but vanish in a busy room, simply by sitting still. He had been dead so long that living people no longer registered him as a presence unless he forced the issue.

"New Amsterdam," Damian said, rubbing the pad of his thumb along the rim of that untasted glass, "has no college of magic. And we have assembled here the beginnings of, if I may be so bold, a rather fine faculty."

"Ah!" Something unknotted inside the wampyr. They wanted something of him—something it would be easy for him to provide. And in return…the beginnings of a court? Or at least the beginnings of those fleeting human friendships that could relieve his tedium. "You wish to secure an endowment?"

They glanced from one to another like guilty children. Damian cleared his throat, but stumbled.

Ruthanna stepped in. "Actually…we were hoping you might agree to teach. Um. Mr. Prior."

Whatever he had thought they were about to suggest, that left him with his mouth hanging open and his hands limp. Undirected in midair. "I beg your pardon?" he said.

"There are *many* schools where a student can go to study about magic," Damian said. "There aren't many where he can study magic with someone who has watched a good bit of it develop."

The wampyr let his hands drop to his knees. "You thought all this up on the airliner?"

Damian smiled. He didn't bother making sure his lips stayed closed. He had a deep voice, a little rough with nervousness as he said, "Only the barest outlines. The details required us all."

"I'll have to think about it. But I will be honest. My initial impulse is to demur." The wampyr raised an eyebrow at the man who pretended to be an immortal. "What do you think, Prince Ragoczy?"

"I think you're trouble," the Prince said. "But you were trouble in the court of Louis the fifteenth, and you were trouble when you outwitted Giacomo Casanova over the dignity of that one lady—what was her name…?"

"Was that me?" the wampyr said, wonderingly. "I thought that was some fanciful hero from an old romance. Something by Dumas, perhaps."

"That was Amédée Gosselin *pére*," said the round-faced man. "Or was it *grand-pére*? The man I knew was Amédée Gosselin *fils*. There's a portrait of the father, you know. Admittedly, the features are lost under a good deal of stylization—but it's not a bad likeness."

The wampyr frowned at the Prince, imagining his slack cheeks and close-cropped hair as they might look beneath a powdered wig. His scent was not familiar, but wampyr had sought to avoid the so-called Comte de St. Germain—in any of his incarnations. Metaphysically-inclined confidence tricksters were the last associates a wampyr who wished to keep a low profile should seek.

He had reason to believe this was not the man. But he had been wrong in his time, and had no reason to believe it could not be so again.

As if aware of the scrutiny, the Prince smiled. "Think about it, Mr. Prior. What we're offering you, after a fashion, is respectability. *Continuity.* No more need to pick up and move every few decades, no more need to reinvent yourself over and over again. You will have a home at our college for all eternity. Universities and churches—what else is that that lasts as long as wampyrs do? Not nations, certainly..."

The wampyr held his face still, feeling—nevertheless— as if this fakir, this fortuneteller, looked right through him and saw his deepest desires.

The Prince continued. "I'm fortunate: no one in a position of real power has ever been quite willing to believe me, so I have had the luxury of telling the truth. But I imagine it cannot be easy for your kind, to drift along so unmoored through the world."

"I'll need to think about it," the wampyr said.

"Of course you will," the Prince answered cheerfully. "Now, Estelle, I have been meaning to ask you about some of the incantations you use..."

"I'll drive you home," Damian offered in the hall much later, as the wampyr was buttoning his coat against the foredawn chill. "It's a long way back to the Hotel Aphatos, and you won't find a cab at this hour."

The wampyr cocked an eyebrow at the taller man. "I am not staying at the hotel."

"Oh," said Damian. "But you implied—"

"I receive messages there," the wampyr clarified, suddenly irritated with himself for withholding information.

"They have been keeping my things. But I have a house. Near the park. I have had it for over sixty years."

"I'll still drive."

With a spread gesture of his hands, the wampyr acquiesced. He wasn't sure exactly when he had lost control of this encounter, but it was almost a novelty, and he found he was not in any hurry to reestablish it.

In the car, Damian said hesitantly, "Which way are you leaning?"

"I have made it a goal to avoid human politics," the wampyr said, his face turned so he could watch the city flicker by outside the windows. Less than twenty-four hours elapsed since he had returned to New Amsterdam.

Damian laughed as if responding to a dry joke—but it trailed off, and he said, "You weren't kidding. But what Ragoczy implied—"

"I try to avoid human politics. That does not mean I can avoid humans."

"I see. And yet you tried to expose Ragoczy as, what, a confidence trickster? How is that not politics? We are not naïve, nor simpletons, Mr. Prior."

"Jack," said the wampyr.

Damian nodded, but did not echo him.

With a sigh, the wampyr said, "If he is lying, he is very good at it. He was right, you know, about what was in Dumas's ridiculous book about Gosselin and what was not. Here, this is the house."

"Ridiculous, was it?" Damian pulled the car over.

The wampyr studied his own fingernails. He reached for the door handle. He stopped. "You are probably in a hurry to get home."

He heard the pause, the consideration. The decision to trust. *Yes, he is a wampyr. Does that mean he is not also an honorable man?*

Damian said, "No one's waiting for me."

That hung between them for a moment, in soft silence and the dry warmth from the automobile's heaters.

"Will you come in to my house, Damian Thomas?" the wampyr asked, with intentional solemnity. He did not care to be mistaken in such things. He was too old for screaming.

Damian paused, hands on the wheel. In a conversational tone, he asked, "How much does it hurt?"

"As I recollect," the wampyr said, "it was most exquisitely pleasurable. But then, my memories of such ancient days are dim."

"I see," said Damian. "You need this?"

"I will not die without it," the wampyr said. "But that I cannot die of starvation does not mean I cannot starve."

The automobile sat idling by the curve for thirty seconds. Ninety.

Damian reached out and turned off the key. "A scientist should always be eager for new experiences," he said.

—⋘—

The wampyr brought the sorcerer up the sweep of his front steps and into that ridiculous foyer. He moved surely in the darkness; the human was hesitant, and not yet accustomed to trusting the wampyr's sure hand on his elbow.

"Where's the light switch?" Damian asked, moving each foot forward as if probing for what he might trip over.

"Not yet installed," the wampyr said. Swiftly, he crossed the room and opened the shades, that the light from the streetlamps might filter in. "I last inhabited this house in 1902. And the gas is turned off, currently."

"I wasn't born yet," Damian said, as if he'd only just started to consider the implications. "When last you were in America."

"When last I was in America," the wampyr said, "The state of New Netherlands was the colony of New Holland, and a British protectorate. If you're going to let that trouble you—"

"I'm just not used to it," Damian said.

His pulse raced with apprehension, anticipation. Curiosity. Not desire—not *yet*, the wampyr judged, but perhaps…

"Trust me," the wampyr said, and led Damian to a settee. It might have looked ridiculous, a man so much smaller pressing one larger to sit, to lean back. To let his head fall against the pillows.

The wampyr let his dry, light hands rest against Damian's shoulders. "I do not usually drink from the throat," he said. "It makes a scar that shows. May I remove your coat?"

Silently, shaking, Damian sat forward. The wampyr slid the jacket from his shoulders, untacked and unknotted his tie, unbuttoned the once-pressed shirt now rumpled with a long day's wear. He laid each article of clothing across the arm of the settee. Damian watched his movements with a focus that told the wampyr his mortal friend saw nothing, now, but a moving patch of darkness in a lesser dark, leavened by reflections from the streetlights.

It might be worse for Damian, being blind. The wampyr could go and find a candle—

But soonest begun was first ended. Even in such dim light, the wampyr had no problem picking out the outlines of Damian's sorcerer's tattoos, though the red ink faded into the darkness of his skin. The wampyr laid his hand against Damian's chest and felt the beat of his heart.

"This will be less…invasive," the wampyr said, "if you lay your arm along the back of the settee."

The sorcerer laughed. "You do realize how ridiculous what you just said is?"

"Or I could sit on your lap," the wampyr said.

Damian laid a hand over his and did not respond directly. "I thought you would be…clammy."

"Cold, sometimes," the wampyr said.

"But I did not think you would feel so…dry."

"You expected a fresh corpse."

"No, I—" His laugh was a nervous hiccough. "Yes. I guess I did. You are—"

"I have been dead," the wampyr said, "since before the Reconquista. Dead and incorruptible. It is what it is."

"I guess so," Damian answered. He touched the wampyr's face. His fingertips were warm, and the pulse of blood thudded through them. "What's it like?"

"The blood?"

"Living forever."

"Nobody else does," the wampyr said, and touched Damian's right hand, with its lonely ring. "You can still leave—"

"I'm stalling," Damian admitted. "Aren't I?"

"I am patient."

"Don't be."

Slowly, still shaking, Damian raised his left arm and laid it along the back of the couch. He turned the palm up and curled his fingers into a fist. He softly curved his right palm around the back of the wampyr's head, twining fingers through his hair.

"Soft," he said, so the wampyr heard his surprise.

The wampyr didn't answer. The rich scent of blood beneath elastic, living skin called to him, sang along his nerves.

The sorcerer sighed. "Do it." His cupped hand followed the wampyr's head down.

He drew a breath as the wampyr's fangs pricked the soft flesh inside his elbow, and as they sank through the skin, his right hand made a fist in the wampyr's hair. "Christ," he muttered, head arching back, as the sweet, thick life filled the wampyr's mouth. "Ow. Ow. Oh, sweet buggered Christ. I *never*—"

His voice broke. He drew a heaving, ragged breath, his heart accelerating under the warm, slightly oily skin where the wampyr rested his own left hand.

"Oh," he said, and fell silent, breathing deeply though pleasure and pain.

# 4.

THE WAMPYR WAS CAREFUL, and took as little as he could bear, as slowly as he could bear. It was hard to stop, with the rush of warmth and life into his body after so long dry and chill and hungry. With the curl of Damian's fingers tight into his hair. But he felt the gooseflesh raise its Braille patterns across Damian's chest, and remembered—the house was cold, for a mortal, and the wampyr had no way to make it warm.

He drew away long before either of them wished him to.

In the normal course of events, the wampyr would have fed Damian afterward—but of course, after sixty years standing empty, there was no food in the house. So he stanched the wound—his fangs were sharp, and the punctures sealed quickly—and wrapped Damian in the sheets that had veiled the settee. The wampyr kissed Damian's moss-springy curls with lips that suddenly tingled with life, and went into the still-dark parlor to fix the sorcerer a drink. To give him a few moments alone, and take a few for himself.

Sometimes they were shamed, shocked. In a hurry to leave. Sometimes so dizzied by unaccustomed pleasures that they would beg to be taken again. When the wampyr was young and inexperienced or had little control, that was when tragedies occurred.

But as the wampyr found glasses—clean, and neatly tidied away in the liquor cabinet—and began sniffing stoppered decanters, Damian slipped up behind him, trailing the sheets like a ghost's funeral shroud.

The wampyr held a brandy bottle over his shoulder, the stopper in his other hand. "Does this smell good to you?"

"It smells fine. I thought wampyrs were supposed to have extraordinary senses."

"I sniffed it through the stopper. It smelled like liquor—which is to say, chemical burns, with an overtone of putrescence. It's hard for me to tell if it has turned." The wampyr poured a third of a glass, then considered Damian's size and tipped in a little more.

"Quel dommage," Damian said, accepting the glass. He sipped and sighed. His gaze followed the wampyr as he extricated himself from between Damian and the liquor cabinet and wandered away across the thick-padded carpet.

Damian said, "Who are you?"

The wampyr permitted himself a flicker of a smile. His flesh tingled as the blood returned to it, bearing sensation and warmth. Keeping his voice light, he answered,

"Etiquette would dictate that that is not the sort of thing one asks the blood."

"Forgive me. I am new at this. Who are you? Other than Jack Prior, and Amédée Gosselin…"

The wampyr snorted. He traced a finger down a leather spine, feeling the texture of embossed hide and gilt. "Those are names. I am a dead man."

The edge of the glass clicked Damian's teeth as he sipped brandy again. "If you do not tell me, I will only invent stories. Each more scandalous than the last."

The wampyr turned. He folded his arms and gazed challengingly up at the sorcerer. "Who are *you*?"

"Damian Thomas. Sorcerer. Both an American and an Englishman. Professor. Teacher. Author. Widower. Occasional—" he huffed in self-amusement. "—civil-rights activist. I have an elderly mother in Deptford. I am also a homosexual."

The hand with the glass in it lowered to his side, no longer raised as a barrier. It was offered vulnerability, like the calm, blatant statement that came before.

"Am I meant to be shocked?" the wampyr said, showing his fangs, letting them catch the dim light from the street.

"Some men would be. Especially since it should be obvious that I find you attractive."

"I am not a man." The wampyr studied Damian's expressions through the darkness, the suppressed muscular twitches he tried to conceal. "You said, widower."

"My wife," Damian said, "was also an academic. And a Lesbian. And a friend. We…"

"Shielded one another?" the wampyr suggested.

"That's a good way of putting it. She had a lover and so did I—" he shrugged. "He is with someone else now."

"I'm sorry," the wampyr said. Eleven or twelve hundred years of experience didn't give you any facile answers as to what the right reply was when someone had just shared a shattering confidence. But there might be something else he could say. Sometimes the right answer to a confidence was simply to reply in kind.

He said, "My name was Lopo, when I was alive."

"Lopo. That's not the sort of name one associates with wampyrs. Shouldn't you have been Count von Something? A Bathory, perhaps? Or at least some ponderous old name with a sinister ring? Vladislav? Gideon? Batholomew?"

"And not the sort of thing you'd call a pet monkey?"

Damian winced theatrically. "I wouldn't have put it just like that."

The wampyr said, "It was the name of an apprentice stonemason. One who was lucky to find the position. His mother had no husband. His father was a Moor who did not keep her. This was in Galicia."

He gestured to his face, aware that to Damian's eyes, the olive tones were lost in the darkness.

"I don't remember it," the wampyr said. It was somehow easier to talk about these things with a virtual stranger—as if he said them to the void, or the night. "I have forgotten so much. But I know...knew...someone older than myself. He told me."

Damian slipped a hand from beneath his sheets and brushed it across the wampyr's face. "You're pale, for a Moor."

The wampyr laughed. Even to his own ear, it had the whispery rasp of an unused door.

"The Berber tribes were Africans, but not all were black Africans. I never knew the man who fathered me, and cannot tell you how he looked—but I can tell you that I was not considered fair as a youth. The blood—we fade, in a thousand years away from the sun. You should see how the old ones get, who were light-skinned in life. Like Grecian marbles, white as ice." He studied his own pale-olive hand. "When I was maintaining the pretense of mortality, a certain swarthiness was an advantage."

The wampyr was not sure what expression lit upon his own face just then, but Damian finished the brandy and hid his face inside the glass for a moment as if enjoying the fumes.

"I suppose I should go," he said as he lowered it. "It will be daylight soon."

The wampyr stepped back, leaving his hand extended for the empty glass. Damian set it in his fingers, letting their skin brush as he did so. It might have been bravado, but that did not mean the wampyr admired it any less.

"I do not," the wampyr said, "retire to a coffin lined with grave-earth at dawn."

"Really?" Damian's forehead wrinkled with amusement. "What do you do?"

"Knit," said the wampyr. "Mostly." When Damian's delighted laughter had subsided, he continued, "You are welcome to stay, but I rather imagine you need your rest."

"I should sleep," Damian said. "But I won't. I have an early train to New Haven, and a class at noon."

"How early?"

"Three hours," Damian said, with a glance at his watch. "I have to return the car; I rented it at the airport." He let the sheets slip from his shoulders. "I suppose I should put my shirt on first."

"Has the bleeding stopped?"

Damian brushed his fingertips across the wound. "Entirely."

His head stayed ducked, his eyes on whatever he could see of the smooth inside of his own elbow through the gloom. One of them had to say it.

"Will I see you again?" the wampyr asked—not meaning *in the company of your charming, ridiculous friends.*

Damian slid the back of his hand against the wampyr's cheek. The wampyr turned to let it brush his mouth. So much warmth, so much life under the dense softness of that skin.

"You have my card," the sorcerer said. "Can I call you?" The wampyr tipped his head. "Once I have installed a telephone."

A housekeeper recommended by the staff at the Hotel Aphatos arrived an hour after sunrise. The first task the wampyr set her was to find out if the household's gas and water could be reconnected. The second was to seek out a reputable electrician for purposes of wiring the house— and for the duration of *that* project, the wampyr would be staying at the hotel.

There were limits to the strength of any man.

Once ensconced in his temporary quarters, the wampyr began the task of integrating himself into New Amsterdam's undead society. It was surprisingly easy: there were still only about two dozen of the blood in New Netherlands, and not all of them came into the city with any regularity. The new openness and ease of travel meant that European wampyrs came and went with relative frequency, and the Hotel Aphatos catered to them—as well as providing a place to meet their local peers.

All he needed to do was sit in the lobby of the Aphatos with a book from the hotel's extensive library on his knee, reading up on the Comte de St. Germain and his alleged six hundred years of history. That was a respectable age even for one of the blood, if you chose to believe he had attained it.

The wampyr was long inured to similar clubs in Europe, but this one had a kind of openness he had not anticipated. *How...American*, he thought, as he watched the young men and women wander in and out, all of them quite obviously knowing exactly what sort of place this was. Outside, in a cold rain, a different set of protestors had gathered.

In the Old World, the wampyr clubs were known by word of mouth among a certain select sort of people. They were not...he hesitated, seeking a phrase...*tourist attractions.*

To think, less than a hundred years before, this young country had been a bastion of Puritanism that had hunted him from its shores for the mere crime of existing, and destroyed one of his offspring in the bargain.

"America," he muttered to himself.

"First time here?" someone said from the next chair over.

He'd known she sat there, of course. No fledgling of twenty or thirty years' development was going to sneak up on someone of his age. But he'd been politely ignoring her, and had expected the same treatment in return.

Then again, he supposed he *had* provided the opening.

"First time since it was the Colonies," he answered, turning on the edge of the chair.

She was a tall, rawboned brunette, the pallor of her cheeks contrasting strikingly with dark, sparkling eyes. Her cheekbones and jaw stretched the taut skin just so, giving the impression of careful engineering.

"Elizabeth," she said.

"I am using Jack," he answered.

"You have many names, I take it."

It was a moment when a mortal might have saluted her with a glass. The wampyr stuck a finger in his book, instead. "And you have only one. But you do not stand on ceremony, so neither shall I."

She smiled. "I'd heard about you. You're the old one, from the continent. They say you're staying."

"My dear," the wampyr countered, "when one is as old as I am, one comes to realize that one never really *stays* anywhere. At most, one can be said, for a time, to alight."

She laughed. It wasn't as good as Estelle Blacksnake's laugh, or even Ruthanna Wehrmeister's. But it was an honest effort, and the wampyr appreciated how hard it was to learn to laugh spontaneously again when one was dead. "We must seem a terribly callow lot to you."

He shrugged. "Are you all brothers and sisters?" The direction of his gaze took in two lovely young men who stood by the rail. They could have been twins, and possibly were, and they had gleaming black hair and a certain strength of nose and jaw line that gave them a resemblance to the young Elizabeth.

"Jamie and Jeffrey are. That is to say, we were made by the same master. At about the same time."

"He—he?—he is young."

"By your standards, aren't we all?" She hooked the waves of her hair behind her ear with a pinkie. "But yes; my creator's name is Zachariah, and *he* was created in Boston around the turn of the century. How did you know?"

He knew of one wampyr who had been in Boston in that era—one other than himself, in any case. *Are you all Epaphras Bull's get, then?* the wampyr wondered. Was all America peopled with his great-grandchildren?

He said, "Only the young make flocks of followers. At my age, most have learned the folly of it."

"Folly?"

"Yes," he said. "One brings another across the veil in order to keep them—well, 'alive' is as similar to what I mean as any word—and close. At my age, one *also* learns how few will remain either of these things for long."

Her fingers rested on his sleeve, her expression stricken. Her flesh was still heavy—the weight of youth. Someday, if she outlived everything she had ever known, she would be as light and dry as he, blown wherever the wind willed it.

He patted her motionless hand to reassure her that he was not offended, and stood. "I beg your pardon," he said. "I just overheard the concierge say my name into the telephone. Say, do you know anything about this fellow in the city who is pretending to be the Comte de St. Germain?"

She looked up at him, but did not rise. "He styles himself Prince Ragoczy?"

The wampyr nodded.

"He comes in all the time," Elizabeth said. "He says its nice to talk to somebody closer to his own age."

The concierge did have a message. He was just setting down his pen when the wampyr approached.

"I beg your pardon. I am Jack Prior. Has anyone called for me?"

Wise in the ways of wampyrs, the concierge showed no surprise. "A Dr. Thomas." He offered the message across his desk.

It was brief and impersonal, amounting to *I hope you will consider our offer seriously, and I look forward to visiting with you again.* The wampyr hid a smile. New Haven was not so far away. The beginnings of a court, already. And in somebody he did not mind talking to.

"Thank you," he said, and tipped the concierge. As he was turning away, however, he became aware that someone by the front doors, where a little light spilled in despite the awnings, was watching him.

Prince Ragoczy, a light overcoat flapping unbelted atop his suit, had paused there in the fall of light with his arms crossed, and was considering the wampyr.

The wampyr raised a hand and waved sardonically.

Ragoczy dropped his arms to his sides and crossed the lobby, hasty strides billowing the skirt of his coat. As he came within human earshot, he said conversationally, "If that wave was any more sarcastic it would be clapping."

"Nonsense," said the wampyr. "Why on earth wouldn't I be thrilled to see you, when our acquaintanceship goes so far back?"

"You really don't remember me." He sighed. "I came to see if I could jog your memory."

"I did not move in the same circles as you claim to have," the wampyr said. "But I will allow you to make your case. Come, perhaps you can convince me."

"And if I do, what do I win?"

"Perhaps you should ask what it is that you lose, if you fail." The wampyr led Ragoczy around the perimeter of the lobby, to the door of the bar.

"I shudder to think. You'll...expose me? Tear my throat out? Toss me to your pack of familiar wolves?"

"Familiars," the wampyr said with a turn of his hand. "Who can afford the vet bills?"

They seated themselves. A self-effacing waitress brought a menu only to Ragoczy, who studied it for a brief moment before ordering a ham sandwich and coffee.

"Well," said the wampyr. "I guess that puts paid to all that speculation that you might be the Wandering Jew."

Ragoczy handed his menu back to the waitress, who withdrew. He swirled the ice cubes in his water glass without drinking. "Or maybe I've relaxed my feelings about Kashrut over the years."

The wampyr arched an eyebrow.

Ragoczy laughed.

The wampyr said, "What I don't understand is what you gain from pretending to immortality."

"Why assume it's a pretense?"

"I know a lot of immortals." The wampyr had a pretty good mastery of the Gallic shrug, even though he was centuries out of practice as a Frenchman. "The majority of them are very invested in keeping the rest of the world from knowing what they are. If you really had the secret of eternal life, you would not advertise—and if you did, the world would be beating a path to your door."

"Why wouldn't I advertise?"

"Because if you did," the wampyr said, "you'd soon have plenty of disgruntled immortals demanding their money back as they discovered how little they liked it. The human spirit, child, is not meant to wear like iron. We are rags, we very old ones, or we are Bodhisattvas, or we are monsters: those are the only outcomes. Be *glad* you are a charlatan!"

It was not the wampyr's way to lose his temper. But now his voice dropped to a furious whisper, and he had to prevent his hands from clenching on the table-edge.

"And even if you were the St. Germain of yore—he too was a petty confidence man. Even Casanova knew him for such. St. Germain was not even a sorcerer, though he claimed to be an alchemist."

"There was a woman with whom we were both acquainted," Ragoczy began. "She spoke of you often. Marie—"

It was the wampyr's turn to laugh, and he did, aglow with true merriment. "I suppose you think I don't know how a cold read works? That's a trick that was old when the Spiritualists relied upon it, Ragoczy. To *think* that I might have been acquainted with a Marie in France. How could you possibly have *known*? Tell me something about myself you could not have learned from books!"

Whatever Ragoczy was about to say next died on his tongue. A newly-familiar scent alerted the wampyr to Damian's approach a second before he heard his footsteps.

"Oh, good," said Damian. "I trust you two are behaving yourselves? Solving the problems of Western society?"

"Perhaps creating a few," the wampyr said. With conscious care, he released the edge of the table and sat back into the stiff embrace of his chair. "Won't you join us?"

*Shouldn't you be resting?* his expression said.

Damian squeezed his knee under the table as he sat. The waitress was back almost instantly, and she withdrew as unobtrusively as before.

"You know," Damian said, perusing the menu, "the scandal of this place isn't that they cater to wampyrs. It's that they let just anybody come in."

The wampyr's head was not bowed over a printed card, so he saw the wrestle of expressions that crossed Ragoczy's face before it settled into perfect bland amusement. Jealousy, sharp and true.

Without raising his gaze, Damian said, "Sarah wanted to let you both know that she wants to talk over some draft ideas for the university charter. She's also got an investor or two lined up."

"I can help with the finances," the wampyr said. *"Only* the finances."

"We'll see."

"We will not." *How easily you commit yourself.* Well, the money was no object, and while he had done many things in all his centuries, he had never founded a university before. He still had no intention of tying himself to this place forever. Or even for a dozen years.

A teacher—what could be more ridiculous? He said so. "I am no sorcerer. Nor teacher of magics."

"You are magical enough for me. Maybe you can teach history."

"Ouch," the wampyr said.

Damian grinned devilishly. He stretched his tall frame against the back of the chair. As if by accident, his legs brushed the wampyr's. "We're meeting tonight at her place. After sundown, of course."

Mercifully, the waitress brought back Ragoczy's sandwich when she returned to take Damian's order. The food gave Ragoczy something to do with his hands and mouth without having to support a conversation—a task that Damian took up quite cheerfully until he, too, was fed. Then it fell to the wampyr, who resorted to the gossip of Prague, six centuries out of date, to keep talk flowing.

Shortly thereafter, Ragoczy excused himself—before Damian had even quite finished eating, and in such haste that he left his newspaper folded beside his napkin. Damian sighed and set his fork across the edge of his plate. He tilted his head to one side and regarded the wampyr with frank appraisal.

"I've realized," he said, "That I need to know what this is."

The wampyr folded his hands. There was really no way to handle this delicately. "You know my kind cannot support…monogamy. It equates to slow murder."

"You'll have other lovers." Damian shrugged. "So may I. I had guessed it was…club rules."

"Love," the wampyr said, "is not always the word for it."

Damian said, "That looked like an uncomfortable conversation I was intruding on. So, even if he's not some immortal Baltic nobleman, what does it harm for him to say so?"

The wampyr realized a moment too late that a mortal man would have shrugged. But he had left it too long, and so he said simply, "He envies you. You should be careful."

"Envies me?"

"He's realized we have an agreement—"

"Jack."

It was that, the wampyr realized—hearing a sound repeated in the voices of people one respected—that made it a name. Otherwise, it was just a dog barking for attention.

"I believe we just established that it is not an exclusive agreement—"

The wampyr cleared his throat, for punctuation rather than of any need. "I fear I am considered somewhat peculiar among my kind. I prefer to limit my depredations to those whose company I enjoy."

Damian straightened his silverware. "I think I'm flattered." But the mind behind his direct, amused gazed was patently aware that *prefer to limit* was not the same thing as simply *limit*.

"He wants to be immortal," the wampyr said as if he were not changing the subject. "Wants it so badly he's convinced himself that he is. And now he wants to convince me."

"So that you will *make* him immortal?" Damian drank water. A crease between his eyebrows deepened, and the wampyr apprehended the shadow of ancient heartbreak as he continued. "Wait. Are you suggesting that you would make me a va—one of the blood? Because, no offense, but we've only just met."

"No," the wampyr said. "But Ragoczy might have convinced himself so."

"Oh," Damian said. He glanced towards the door.

"We're not immortal. We are just unputrefying—at least, until it all gets too much for us." The wampyr snapped his fingers by way of illustration. "Then, fzzt!"

"It's not possible he's really St. Germain?"

The wampyr smiled sadly. "Do you know how many St. Germains I have met? Every one of them wants to be someone he is not."

"And he did not know you?"

"I lied," the wampyr said. "There was a Monsieur Gosselin in Paris contemporaneous with Giacomo Casanova and the alleged St. Germain, who claimed to be a son of the famous wampyr hero of Louis Quatorze's court. But it was not me. It was..." he waved a hand in the direction that Ragoczy had taken "...an impersonator, if you will."

"Huh," said Damian. "I never before fully appreciated the drawbacks of being a culture hero." He ate a few more bites of pasta. "I don't care what Ragoczy thinks. Am I being too forward for *you*?"

The wampyr steepled his fingers. "Anyone you shock in the Hotel Aphatos came here to be shocked."

# 5.

WHILE DAMIAN FINISHED HIS dinner, the wampyr reached across the table to retrieve Ragoczy's abandoned copy of the *Manhattanite*. It was a full-sized paper, not the tabloid he had anticipated. When he flipped it open, though, his fingers stuck against the surface as if it were printed on fly paper.

He had anticipated a grainy, flare-daubed, underexposed print from his flight from the cameras on the previous morning. Instead, his fingertips brushed the stark, exquisite jaw of a young woman whose pallor and stern bearing made her seem a heroic, martial statue hewn of ice. She did not look a day over seventeen.

She wore a plain traveling suit in some fabric that read grey on film, but it might as well have been a uniform. In the photograph, her hair seemed white where it bounced against broad shoulders. The wampyr knew it was ice-blonde, though. As his fingertips traced those pale waves, he felt the stillness of the hunt steal over him. Expression dropped from his face; he felt the effort it took to maintain the semblance of humanity slip away.

Gently, he turned the paper, and read the caption that lay above the fold.

**Former Sturmwolfstaffel Hauptsturmführerin Ruth Grell arrives at the New Amsterdam Port Authority on Tuesday evening.**

Above her face, the headline screamed across three columns:

Prussian Wolf In America

He flipped to below the fold and read of the controversial—nay, *notorious*—Captain Grell, an English Jew who some said had gone into the service of the enemy, and who some said had infiltrated their innermost ranks until she became a member of the Prussian Chancellor's personal guard—whereupon she had led a successful assassination plot against him and several of his top advisors.

She had stood trial in Prussia, and been condemned to an extermination camp as a traitor, a Jew, and a Lesbian—but the sentence had not come to its inevitable fruition before the end of the war. Whereupon she had stood trial in Nuremburg, and been acquitted, in large part because of testimony recorded against her in her Prussian trial by a woman the wampyr knew had been her lover, Sturmwolfstaffel Obersturmführerin Adele

Kneeland. Grell had never said as much to anyone, even as Lieutenant Kneeland condemned her—and Kneeland had refused to testify at the second trial. She'd been sentenced to a prison term for her service to the Prussians, but had only served a half-year of it before she was deemed a conscript under new rules and pardoned for her not particularly serious crimes. She'd spent her war in Berlin, and had taken no part in the storied atrocities of the Prussian horde.

As far as the wampyr had heard, Kneeland was living out a quiet retirement in Tsarist Germany, which was Prussia no longer. He had lost track of Captain Grell, as she must have intended, despite an offer he had once left with her to come and find him when the war was done.

The court of public opinion was still divided, as far as the wampyr knew. Captain Grell was a Mata Hari; Captain Grell was a war hero; Captain Grell was no better than she should be—and perhaps a Hell of a lot worse. But the wampyr knew a few old soldiers—ones who had fought the front lines on both sides of the Great War, enduring mustard gas and artillery and the thunder of armored cavalry rolling across battlefields strewn with broken men.

He rather thought those men would have sent her white roses every day, if they knew where to find her.

There were no quotations from Captain Grell in the paper. Apparently she had met the reporters at dockside with a thousand-yard stare in her pale blue eyes and a battle-honed "No comment."

"Oh, Ruth," he said.

The story was continued inside. Seeking the rest of it—hoping and dreading another photo—the wampyr flipped the first page. Only to find a different story, albeit one of equal concern, at the top of page three.

Apparently Abby Irene's obituary was running in the society pages because there was a note to that effect below a much clearer photograph of himself than he would have anticipated, annotating a story about his arrival in New Amsterdam that was only a little less sensationalistic than the one featuring Ruth. The wampyr had underestimated the state of the art in telephoto lenses.

Damian could not have missed his distraction. "Jack?"

"Once we moved quietly," the wampyr said. He turned the paper so Damian could read the article about his arrival. He let the article about Ruth stay hidden.

"Now the paparazzi follow you." Damian gave him an encouraging smile. "Look, I have some errands—"

"Go," said the wampyr. "I will meet you at Sarah's home tonight."

"Yes," said Damian. He stood, and was gone before the wampyr noticed that he had left money to cover the cost of his meal.

Ragoczy, of course, had not done so. But the newspaper would suffice.

One of the delights of modern life, the wampyr decided, was that he did not need to wait for a rainy day to take care of the sort of inquiries normally handled during business hours. Instead, he availed himself of one of the hotel's telephones and made a few calls.

His new status as a public figure was a mixed blessing in his old profession. It would be a challenge to create the sort of network of informants and acquaintances so essential to a private detective's work. And there were those in law enforcement and its associated disciplines who were not...sanguine...about wampyrs. But in general, the police were more educated than general society when it came to the existence and habits of the blood.

Prejudice aside—and they had plenty—they had a vested interest in knowing who the killers were.

And the wampyr *did* still have an extensive network of contacts in London, in Moscow, and elsewhere. These included the grandson of a Moscow homicide detective to whom the wampyr had once been very close indeed.

The long-distance bill would be substantial. But in the end, and far more easily than anticipated, the wampyr had the information he required.

The wampyr left the Aphatos at sunset, while red banners still crept from behind the buildings concealing the western sky.

It must have been shift change for the protestors, because there seemed to be about twice as many as there had before. Perhaps, like their prey, they turned out at nightfall.

*Their prey.* Hah.

The young wampyr he'd met earlier, the lovely Elizabeth, loitered against a lamppost clad in blue jeans and a black cowhide jacket, stiff with age and scuffed at the elbows so the rich dry scent still rose from the leather. Heavy boots encased her calves, and the faint smell of gasoline surrounding her hinted that she'd arrived on a motorcycle. She was not smoking a cigarette, but she held one theatrically. The wampyr understood that it was a part of her costume.

He had nothing but approval for this modern phenomenon of women in trousers…and tight ones at that. She caught his eye. He nodded, aware as he did so that she would cultivate him for his age—his experience, his status, his power—as much as for anything about him that might genuinely interest her. But friends were precious, friends were rare—so he nodded as she walked towards him, her hair tossed down her back.

One of the protestors stopped to catcall, and she turned and gave him the finger. The wampyr would have warned her against giving them any notice, inviting them into the circle of her attention. But he was too late, and then there was a crest of noise like a breaking wave—

He saw just the one escort, and the doorman in red, and there were perhaps ten of the young men with signs. Worse, two or three girls had joined them, and men with women watching were not prone to back down. He and Elizabeth were the only blood outside, and as the thud of her hard rubber soles came closer, he saw her bitten lip as she realized her error. Someone shouted something vile; he held her gaze, willing her not to turn. Willing her to come to him. If he could reach her, bring her inside—

They could survive a mob scene, and probably even protect the doorman and the escort. But the Hotel Aphatos might not survive the publicity that would follow if any of the protestors were hurt. And the legal status of the blood in America was always precarious.

Elizabeth covered the last three steps between them. He reached out to take her shoulder—

His left hand rose reflexively. When it descended, his fingers were curled around a broken chunk of pink granite cobblestone. A souvenir, no doubt, wrested from one of New Amsterdam's ancient side streets. And hurled with pathetically inadequate but lethal intent by one of those clean-cut young men.

The wampyr weighed it in his hand. Rounded on one side, jagged on the other. About the size of a cricket ball, and heavier. He ran a thumb against one of the facets; the dry ridges of his skin caught.

The noise of the jeering crowd redoubled as he raised his eyes and his left hand.

"Your aim," he said, "is poor."

The stone cracked in his hand. Cleanly in two, with a little sifting of sand. He let the smaller part fall before the larger, so they hit *one-TWO*.

In the silence that followed, he took Elizabeth's elbow and escorted her inside. She walked boldly until the door shut behind them, but he could feel her leaning against him. As soon as they were concealed by the screens, she turned to him and said, "Even for one of the blood—"

"The stone," he said calmly, "was flawed. A crack, probably from when it was broken with the hammer. *You* could have shattered it."

Her eyes widened. Her lips tightened.

She began to laugh, one hand on a pillar for support, just as if she really needed the breath she was wasting.

Discretion and valor being what they are, the wampyr asked to be shown a more discreet exit from the hotel. He considered hailing a cab, but given how lucky he'd gotten the previous morning it seemed like presuming upon the fates, especially since cabdrivers appeared from his limited sample to favor the *Manhattanite*. So he hid his face behind a scarf he did not need and ventured into the subways.

They were quick and efficient and none too clean, and having misread the map, he found himself on the wrong line—ascending the western edge of Jardinstraat rather than the east. It was easily enough remedied: he alighted, ascended, then transected the park along the route 89th Street would have followed had it been permitted to continue.

He did not trouble himself with paths, but merely skirted the southern edge of the reservoir. He knew the location of the house. And he was starting to get the lay of the land in this strange New Amsterdam.

Whoever was following him stayed downwind and moved quietly, but the wampyr's hearing was keen. It wasn't the patter or crunch of footsteps that revealed a stalker, but the pattern of silences in the cries of night birds, newly returned to the city with the onrushing spring.

So he played the game through the dark, waiting for the eddy that would carry him a scent. At first, the wampyr wondered if the stalker thought he in turn was hunting, like some storybook fiend, and meant to stop him—but then the scent came, familiar, the musk of a beast and the sweetness of a girl, and he relaxed.

The moon was waning now, but only just. A predator's eyes shone in the dark with amplified light; a wampyr's were no exception, and those reflections helped him see. He stopped in a meadow where the moon shadows lay like ink on the withered grass and turned back along his own path with folded arms.

„Obersturmführerin," he called, softly enough so only a monster's ears would hear him. „Why don't you come out of the darkness?"

Ruth Grell appeared before him like a shadow in reverse, her pale skin and hair silhouetted against the darkness behind her as she let her concealing wine-red velvet hood slide down. The wampyr knew it was velvet; he heard the nap rustle across the space that separated them.

"English," she said. "And please do not call me that, Dr. Chaisty."

"If you promise not to call me Dr. Chaisty."

She smiled, a lovely child, and drifted like a stalking wolf across the distance between them. The shell she wore had not aged a day since he met her in 1938. And yet what lived inside was a woman now, a warrior, and not a babe courageous beyond measure and determined to save—or avenge—her family. "All right, Dracula. That was what we settled on last time, wasn't it?"

"Call me Jack. And I shall call you—Miss Grell?"

"Ruth," she said.

He said, "Ruth. How did you find me?"

She touched the side of her nose. Her fingernails were thick and long, as clear as glass. She had filed them to elegant ovals. "I tracked you from the Aphatos. You said once…"

As if her throat had closed up around the words, she shook her head and looked down.

"I told you to find me when the war was over, and you were alone."

"If I lived."

"You lived."

She was warm in the icy darkness. Steam rose from her words; none from his. Her chest rose and fell with the breathing. His lay still until he worked it like a bellows to push out the words.

She said, "Are you so sure?"

"Transformation is not death." He placed a cold hand on her cheek. "Take it from me."

"Heh." It wasn't a laugh so much as a soft huff. She folded her arms and leaned back against a tree. "So what is it like?"

"Transformation?"

"I've done that." Bright hair whisked across the collapsed hood. "Death."

"It hurts," he said. *And what is it about this return to this city that demands confidences of you, left and right?* "There's the pleasure, of course. And after the pleasure, the pain. And then a spiral, a cold vortex, pulling you down…until you awaken again, starving, with fire in every vein. Even the dark is too bright, and even the night is too loud. And if you are very, very fortunate…your creator is there to receive you, and explain what has happened, and what happens next."

She said, "*Barukh atah Adonai Eloheinu melekh ha-olam, ha-gomeyl lahayavim tovot sheg'malani kol tov.*"

He said, "All places shall be Hell, that is not Heaven."

She came and linked her arm in his, and said, "Some old monster you turned out to be. Come and walk a while with me."

He let her lead him among the dark, and waited while she thought about what she wanted to say. *Aphatos indeed*, he thought, but eventually she found the words.

"Did you know I'd live forever? When you made that offer?"

"No one lives forever," he said. "But I suspected you might endure for a long time. You and the other Sturmwölfe."

"You," she said. "You change your name. You move from place to place. You are a vagabond. Is that from fear of what they would do to you?"

*Yes.* "Some of my kind have found other answers." *Divorcing themselves utterly from human society, but for their courts. Cultivating a family, a dynasty to feed them in exchange for riches or protection. Hunting by night, without remorse. Setting themselves up as demon-kings, and taking tribute where they would.*

*Walking into the daylight. Walking into the fire.*

He swallowed it all and said, "Nothing is eternal, Ruth."

"Well," she said. "The sorrowful fate of the Thousand-Year Reich proves you right. But this…abnegation of yours. This denial of continuity of experience? It *can't* be good for you."

"It isn't."

"But it keeps you alive?"

"I am not," he said, "precisely speaking, alive."

Her fingers tightened in the crook of his elbow. "I have no one but you. I am a war criminal. Ulfhethinn. A monster. The others like me—" she shrugged "—they are, or were, Prussian beasts. They hate me. They would hunt me as a dog hunts the wolf that slew its master."

"We are monsters together." He laid his cold fingers over her warm ones. "I don't avoid politics because the world won't change. I avoid them because it always changes back."

"Do you think I did a bad thing?"

"I think you did a beautiful thing," he said. "A task that, not being Sisyphus, one creature can only perform so many times before exhaustion wears her thin."

"I want to see the world," she said. "I want to be someone other than Ruth Grell, traitor."

"You want me to come with you."

She squeezed. The scents of the city night surrounded them as they rounded the edge of the reservoir: icy water, leaf mold, asphalt, exhaust, a whiff of gasoline. "Have you ever killed a man?"

He said, "You've only done it the once."

"Yes."

"It won't get easier. Not until you learn to desire it, as some do."

"It's not a man's death I desire."

"No," he said. "It's a woman's love. And you cannot have that either. Find someone else. Someone who has not sworn fealty to a worse monster than either of us. Find someone better. Love her."

"First," she said, "I thought I'd see if I could find a friend."

He squeezed her hand again. Her grip was so tight on his sleeve that his clasp did not bend her fingers. "You can't run from your demons, Ruth."

"They have wings," she whispered.

"And it attracts their attention." He winked at her in the moonlight. She laughed, just a little.

"Come with me."

"Maybe," he said.

"You say you despise politics," Ruth said. "And here you are, maintaining an identity as a wampyr in a city where that's an act of public defiance. An act of politics, *Jack*."

"I'm not doing it to change the world."

"You're tired." She let her fingers fall from the crook of his arm. "I'm tired too."

"You have," he said, "as yet no frame of reference for how tired it is possible to become."

He wasn't sure what he'd said to anger her, but her spine stiffened and her heart beat harder as the warmth collapsed into her core. "Then just walk into the sun," she snarled. "Have the courage for suicide, if you're done with existing. Don't stand around waiting to be killed! Or do you think anybody will care about a *vampire* martyr? Either kill yourself, or get your teeth back into the world. But choose one!"

She had done what she had done. And he believed she had been justified, even heroic, in doing it. But it was hard, so hard, not to listen to the voices saying otherwise. And unlike him, she had no models on how to live a thousand years with the worm of doubt gnawing your gut, and the regrets drifting around one's foundations like snow.

"Ruth—"

The explosion interrupted him. Blue-silver, a gas fire, shuddering up behind the trees across Jardinstraat, climbing the night.

"Mein Gott," she said, with the forgetfulness of long programming. "What is *that*?"

"It *was* my house," he said.

# 6.

SHE STARED AT HIM, seeming not to understand those words in his calm, almost bemused tone. "Your *house*? We have to—"

"There should have been no one inside. And there are the sirens of the fire brigade." Faintly, a rising wail floating on the moist cool air. "Somebody wishes me to understand that I am not welcome here."

"We have to do something."

"It's things," he said. He touched her shoulder. "Just things, Ruth. And a beautiful old building, which can be rebuilt." *Things. Jack's things.*

Perhaps someone had done him a favor.

"You can find me at the Aphatos," he said. He let his hand fall away; she scarcely seemed to notice. "I recommend the side door."

— ❧ —

He was late, perhaps a little more so than was fashionable, but—just—within the bounds of etiquette for an informal gathering. The others were already assembled, and as Miss Emrys—Sarah—led him into the now-familiar library, Damian was checking his watch.

It left a sense of satisfaction.

No matter how old one got, it was always gratifying that someone cared enough to worry.

"I'm sorry I was delayed," the wampyr said, unable to resist. "My house blew up."

Unable to resist, perhaps. But he *should* have resisted, because a second explosion followed, though this one was composed of questions and not a little fussing.

"It's all right," the wampyr assured them, taking the seat they had left open. "No one was injured, to my knowledge, and the fire brigade seems quite competent to contain the damage. And it's not as if it's the first time—well, the first time for that residence, true."

He'd had a house burned around him, once, but he wasn't about to mention that here. Nor did he particularly care to recollect it, or the long and terrible process of healing. He had been far from help, far from others of his kind, young—by the standards of the blood—and callow.

He was not proud of what he had done in the time that followed.

Some of that history must have permeated the silence that followed, or perhaps it was just the wampyr's calm that made Ragoczy's cup rattle in his saucer. The expression on his face was quite gratifying, before he hid it behind the porcelain rim. As with the crystal, the china was mismatched, and as with the china, the effect was charming.

The putative Comte de St. Germain was trying for an aspect of bland sangfroid…but the wampyr could make out the tremor along his upper lip and the way his scent soured with fear. *There you have it, my dear Count. What it means to be what the world thinks of as "immortal."*

In the awkward silence that followed, Ruthanna toasted him with her teacup—red cabbage roses quite overwhelming tiny violets, and a speckled gold rim. "We were just arguing over whether we should expect you, Jack. I am sad to say I doubted you."

"Really?" He perched on the edge of the wooden chair, feeling unmoored. "I shall not ask who my defenders were. In any case, I am here now, and prepared to discuss the necessities—and the niceties—of arranging a foundation that can support your university."

Estelle glanced at Damian, who had cleared his throat ever so slightly. She did not smile, exactly, as he made a gesture of handing something over to her. His hands were surprisingly graceful for those of such a large man.

She said, "What do we have to do to make you reconsider your role?"

"Please," the wampyr said. "I—"

He stopped, arrested not by Estelle's frown but by the still-fresh memory of Ruth Grell's face painted in unearthly colors by the flames.

"I am still considering," he said. "I am considering, in point of fact, if I am going to remain in New Amsterdam at all."

Damian started from the settee, and Ruthanna set her cup aside as well. "Jack—"

The wampyr raised an eyebrow.

"Talk to me," Damian said, rising the rest of the way. "In the kitchen." He glanced at Sarah. "We'll get some more tea?"

"Of course," Sarah said smoothly. "Use the blue pot."

The wampyr allowed Damian to usher him down the hall with every evidence of meekness. He leaned against the wall while Damian, obviously familiar with the kitchen, filled the kettle and lit the gas. The flames were as blue as the ones that had consumed the house on Jardinstraat.

"If this is too much for you," the wampyr said, while Damian warmed the teapot and measured tea, "I understand quite fully."

Damian laughed. He raised his face to the heavens and shook it from side to side in incredulous wonder. "Jack... this is not the first time a friend's house has been fire-bombed. I am not looking for an escape. I was concerned about *you*. Are you really going to let them drive you out of the city?"

"Back into the wilderness?" the wampyr said. "I had not thought of it in those terms, or how it would appear—"

"Then what," asked Damian, "was your motivation?"

"An old friend." The wampyr idly picked the dry, hard skin of a fingertip with his opposite hand. "She wishes me to come traveling with her."

"Another wampyr?"

Damian hid the jealousy well as he poured the first warm water out of the teapot and flushed it down the drain, replacing it with rounded spoons of dried leaves as the kettle began to sing. Well, but not well enough to fool the wampyr.

"A wolf," the wampyr said. "What would you have me do, then, Damian?"

"I've known you for two days. I'm not sure I get to have an opinion."

"But you do."

Damian clicked the flame off and poured the boiling water. Aromatic steam rose from the leaves as he wet them.

"Opinions are like kittens," he commented. "People are always giving them away."

"I'm asking."

Damian turned, folding his arms, his back to the white enamel stove which clicked as it cooled. "I'd stand and fight, if it were me."

"You do. In point of fact."

That drew a smile. "What better way to make students see a wampyr as a...well, as not so much a monster, than to *teach* them?"

"Damian," the wampyr said softly. "I *am* a monster, my dear."

In the time it took for the tea to be made, the party had drifted from its mooring in the library. Now Estelle and Ruthanna were engaged in some erudite argument about the nuances of spellcasting while Sarah played referee. Meanwhile, Ragoczy had taken his teacup and saucer into the parlor and seated himself on the leathern bench of a powder-blue bentside spinet tucked into a corner there.

The wampyr touched Damian on the sleeve in the hall, relieved him of the teapot, and made his way past the glass partition into the parlor.

"Tea?" he asked, when Ragoczy looked up.

"Thank you." Ragoczy removed his cup from the sideboard and held it well away from the harpsichord so the wampyr could pour without endangering the instrument's finish. He sipped, and set the cup back in the saucer.

"If I were cruel," the wampyr said, "I would grant your wish."

"My wish?"

"To be immortal, Nykyfor Borysovich. Or the nearest approximation there is."

It was a good thing Ragoczy had set the tea down, given the way the keys of the spinet rattled under his fingers. "Where on earth—"

"My kind have been shedding our old selves and reinventing new ones for millennia. And we know how to find each other. You...are only human, Gospodin Kiroff." The wampyr said it softly, like a benediction. "So, how fortunate for you that I am not cruel. Merely selfish."

Ragoczy lifted his chin, like a maiden in a romance. "You will not help me."

"You would think it help, for a little while." The wampyr shook his head. "No. You will have to find your Philosopher's Stone without me...'Prince Ragoczy.'"

Ragoczy drew himself up and in, so the wampyr could imagine the armor assembling. "Who are you to make that decision for me?"

"I am making it for myself," the wampyr said. "Call it selfishness. And a little charity. If you do not love yourself, as you are now, my dear Ragoczy, how little will you love yourself when a hundred years have refined you that much closer to your core?"

When the party ended, there was dark enough left that the wampyr decided to seek out Ruth Grell again. Dark enough, he thought. Inside and out.

He did not know where she would be, so he found the place in the park where he had left her. She was long gone, but he crouched by the roots of the tree she had leaned against and closed his eyes. He pressed his cold hand to the cold soil and sniffed deeply.

When he opened his eyes again, he smiled. "Can I not find a wolf in this city?"

He followed the scent like a hound—like a wolf—across the too-perfect squares of cement and the scraps of dirty ice that had collected in corners from the day's melt. He followed her between the blown sandwich-wrappers and the cardboard pallets of the homeless, down the Boston Post Road and the channels of the gutter.

He found her on a rooftop. Beyond the streetlights, the sky was growing shallow with false dawn, but though he could sense it, he could not see it.

"You shouldn't be here," Ruth Grell said, without turning, from her seat on the parapet wall. "It's rising morning."

"Hours yet," he answered. It was only a slight exaggeration. He hitched a leg over the parapet and sat beside her.

"So," he said, when a few moments had passed. "Will you accuse me of cowardice now?"

"Have you made up your mind who to be?"

He shrugged, this time with slow intent. "I had thought you might help me decide."

"It's easier," she said, "when there is someone you very much would rather not be."

He didn't answer. She touched his shoulder, finally, which was a good thing. It roused him from all those remembrances of all the people he had decided not to be, anymore.

He said, "Will you stay in New Amsterdam?"

"It was a long trip to come here," she said. "But there are many places I have not been. And I..." She glanced away, coloring across the high bones of her cheeks. The flush warmed her skin. Her pulse speeded.

"Finances?"

"Not everyone has a lot of use for a retired Sturmwolfstaffel Hauptsturmführerin," she said. "And there wasn't much of a pension."

He rubbed a fingertip across the gritty cement of the parapet. "Wherever you want to go," he said, "I can pay for it."

She would have said his name in protest, but she didn't know what name to say.

"Don't worry," he said. "Money is no object. Consider it the just thanks for a grateful world for your service."

She frowned. She stared.

He continued, "You can travel as you wish, and come back here. Or Paris. Or San Diego; it was lovely when I visited there with Abby Irene and Phoebe, and they will not still hold the war against you the way the English Americas will. There are wild hills for a wolf to run in—"

She was not a shapeshifter, not like the werewolves of the stories. Rather, she was a creature out of a different legend, one of the Ulfhethnar. A wolf-shirt, a kind of mystic warrior. It did not make her any less a wolf clothed in woman's mind and woman's skin.

"The sun—" she said, changing the subject.

He shrugged. "What of it?"

The sideways glance she gave him was stricken. "You don't mean it."

"I don't know," he said. It occurred to him that with those words, he made himself more vulnerable to her than he had allowed himself to be to anyone in a millennium. Since he left Evie, his creator, or since Evie left him. He didn't remember.

But he remembered her dark hair, and the flash of her Mediterranean eyes. And the cold strength of her arms' embrace.

She'd chosen to burn. And such was the nature of things that he had not even known, until too much later.

Perhaps he could be so honest with Ruth because she was a monster too, and an equal, but not competition. And not something to be protected.

"You said, if I wanted to, I should have the courage to do it directly."

"I did," she admitted, after her mouth closed on the protest she was too honest to give voice to. "Do you want to?"

"I promised somebody I wouldn't. As long as he remained." He took a breath he didn't need. "So he wouldn't be alone."

"And he's remained?"

The wampyr shrugged. "I don't know. I haven't seen him since."

"Ouch." She took his hand and squeezed, a grip so strong he allowed himself to squeeze back. Her smooth nails curled against his palm. "You didn't answer. Do you want to?"

He shrugged. The sky shimmered silver behind the lights. Faint trails of peach and gold glowed beyond the city, beyond the water. "If I go inside, I guess I don't."

"Well." She turned away and slipped her hand from his. With a graceful jump, she rose to her feet on the parapet. "I've rented a room on the fourth floor. I'm sure you can find it. I'm not going to sit here and watch you die so you can prove to yourself how lonely you are."

"Touché," he said, rising too. He followed her across the roof, to a steel door she'd propped open.

They slipped inside with the draft. Opalescent eye-shine—oranges and golds—filled her wide-blown pupils. Her head jerked back.

"Violet," she said, when he tilted his own in a question. "Your eyes. In the dark."

"Yours are the color of fire opals...I said something wrong?"

"No." She shook her head, smoothed her crumpled expression. Her intonation military, she continued, "Adele's were green."

"Oh," he said. "I'm sorry."

"So'm I," she said. "I'm acting like nobody else has ever lost anybody."

He took her arm. "Show me your room," he said. "And I'll tell you about Evie."

She had sense enough not to answer, but just to lead him in silence down the stairs. As they descended, in a lighter tone, he said, "This has proved a useful exercise in one way."

"Oh?" she said.

"It's proven to me that I'm not staying in this city because of a deathwish. If you can call it that, in one already dead."

"They blew up your *house*—"

"So?" he interrupted. "One should refuse to do something worthwhile because it's dangerous?"

Sturmwolfstaffel Hauptsturmführerin Grell had, as he had suspected, no answer for that.

At nightfall, the wampyr returned to the Aphatos. He meant to dress, perhaps dine, and find a way to spend the dark hours until another morning. He reckoned without Ruthanna and Damian, though, and the plainclothes policeman sitting beside them in the lobby, behind the screens and out of line of sight to the protestors—but where he would have to walk past them to reach the lifts.

He didn't bother to avoid them. He was disheveled, he knew, and not nearly the picture of precision in dress and grooming he preferred to present. It didn't matter. He lighted on the edge of the divan opposite and offered up his hand.

Even the detective shook it, with no more than an involuntary show of distaste. Damian introduced him as Detective Travis Young; the wampyr was struck most by his eyebrows, black and arched like a gull's taut wing. "I'm sorry to ambush you like this, but, as you are probably aware, NAPD is investigating the firebombing of your house, Mr. Prior, and we were hoping you'd make yourself available to answer a few questions."

"My night is yours," the wampyr said. "Once I have a word with my friends."

Detective Young shifted uncomfortably on the edge of the too-soft chair. "Mr. Thomas mentioned that you might have plans to leave town—"

"Actually," the wampyr interrupted. "I have decided to accept a position that he and Dr. Wehrmeister had offered me. So no, I will be available to your inquiries." He let his mouth twitch up into a smile. "Barring more successful assassination attempts."

"You'll stay?" Damian said, clasping his hands in his lap.

"I'll stay."

Ruthanna sighed as if released from pain. Had it really meant so much to her? "We're glad you saw your way clear to join us. It's an incredibly brave and selfless act, all things considered—"

"I'm not doing it for you," the wampyr said, as kindly as he could. *I'm doing it because an old friend would have thought it was the right thing to do.* He looked at Detective Young, who was edging away. "It's fine," the wampyr said. "None of this is private."

He caught Damian quietly beaming, though, and wondered if it was dishonest to let him think he was staying because it was the right thing to do. Maybe he was. Self-delusion was not a vice limited to the living.

He waited a few moments, to see if the mortals would speak, and when they did not, he continued, "I think I do not care to be remembered forever as Jack Prior."

Ruthanna said, "How shall we list you on the charter, and as faculty, then? Not as Amédée Gosselin?"

Damian's lips writhed into a grin. *Lopo Cantero?* He mouthed. The wampyr rolled his eyes, but made a note: apparently his new friend spoke some Spanish.

He answered, "I should like to be recorded as Sebastien de Ulloa."

Ruthanna's brow wrinkled with surprise. "That's a notorious name."

"Nevertheless," said the wampyr. "I think I should like to be him. He had excellent friends."